The Storm

Written by Victoria Harris

Illustrated by Brigid Malloy

The Storm

Victoria Harris

Paperback Edition First Published in Great Britain in 2022 by Ogham Publishing
Copyright © Victoria Harris 2022

Illustrated by Brigid Malloy

Disclaimer

This is a work of fiction. Names, characters, businesses, places, events and incidents are either the products of the author's imagination or used in a fictitious manner. Any resemblance to actual persons, living or dead, or actual events is purely coincidental.

ISBN: 978-1-9196126-1-4
Ogham Publishing

For the Adventurer

Once there was a badger called Benny. He lived in the most beautiful forest in the world. At least, he thought so. There were tall, strong trees with lots of green leaves, streams and ponds, big rocks and even a few hills. Best of all, there were lots of friendly animals.

Sometimes it rained, and every once in a while it snowed. But most of the time, the forest was a bright, sunny place.

Benny lived in an underground home, called a sett, with his family. His parents kept themselves very busy digging tunnels, searching for food and collecting soft grass for their beds.

Benny enjoyed playing outside. His favourite place to play was a little glade surrounded by trees and filled with wildflowers. He spent almost every day there with his best friend Sammy, a squirrel.

One day, there was a big storm. Benny huddled at home with his family, trembling every time he heard the big BOOM of thunder.

'Don't be scared, Benny,' said his mother. 'Thunder can't hurt you.'

But Benny couldn't help it. Every time the thunder went BOOM, his heart started beating too fast and his stomach went *flip-flop*.

BOOM

He wasn't just afraid, he was embarrassed too. Why did thunder scare him so much? Benny remembered one time he'd been playing in the glade with Sammy. They were having so much fun, and they didn't notice the storm clouds overhead. All of a sudden, there was a big BOOM of thunder, and Benny jumped up into the air! Sammy had laughed and laughed. Benny had tried to laugh too. But honestly, he felt silly for being so scared.

Benny hid underground as deep as he could go. But he could still hear the thunder.

BOOM went the thunder.

Thump-thump-thump! went Benny's heart.

Flip-flop! went Benny's stomach.

Over and over and over again.

'Is this storm ever going to end?' asked Benny at last.

'It is a big one, Benny,' said his mother, peering out of the sett.

'The biggest one I've ever seen,' said his father.

That did not make Benny feel any better. It didn't answer his question either.

The next day the storm was still raging. Benny's parents dug tunnels, hunted for food and gathered grass as if everything was normal. But Benny didn't feel everything was okay. He was tired of feeling scared every time he heard a BOOM! At least three times, he asked his parents:

'When will the storm end?'

And every time, he got the same answer.

'All storms end sooner or later.'

That didn't answer Benny's question. In fact, it made him worry even more. Finally, he decided to ask Ollie, the owl who lived near the glade. Ollie was the wisest creature in the whole forest. He must know when the storm would end!

Benny crawled out of the sett and headed to
the glade. The whole forest looked different!
Everything was wet and muddy. Big branches had
fallen off the trees and lay broken on the ground.
A few trees had also fallen over, including the
one Sammy lived in with his family. Benny got a
fright. His mouth felt dry and his heart heavy.

When he reached the glade, he gasped. The whole area was flooded! The flowers were gone, swallowed up by muddy water. Benny wanted to cry.

'Ollie? Ollie, are you here?'

'Hello, Benny.'

Benny looked up and saw the owl in a tree. 'Ollie, I'm worried about my friend Sammy! His family's tree fell over in the storm!'

Ollie sighed. 'I know. Many squirrels lost their homes last night in this terrible storm. But don't worry, they are safe! They've moved to a place beyond the hill.'

Benny was relieved to know Sammy was safe. But the fact that Sammy had moved away made his heart hurt. This storm was ruining everything!

'Ollie! When will this storm end?' Benny asked.

Ollie blinked his wide yellow eyes. He tilted his head left, and then to the right. Benny waited for the answer.

'I don't know,' he said at last.

Benny stared at him in disbelief. 'But you know everything!'

'I know a great deal,' Ollie replied. 'But not everything is knowable.'

Benny did not like this answer one bit.

BOOM!

Benny leapt up high in the air at the clap of thunder. His heart went thump-thump-thump. His stomach went flip-flop. 'I wish everything could be the same again,' he cried.

Ollie blinked. 'Did you say wish?'

'Yes,' Benny said. 'Why?'

'Well, there's a magic wishing tree deep in the forest!'

Benny smiled for the first time since the storm had begun. 'Really? If I find it, will it grant my wish?'

'Hmm.' Ollie looked thoughtful. 'It will grant you the wish that you need. It may not grant the wish that you want.'

Benny had no idea what Ollie the wise meant. He needed as well as wanted everything to go back to normal.

'How do I find the magic tree?'

Ollie gestured with his wing.

'That is the path that will lead you to the magic tree. Although you may find the journey difficult, because of this storm.'

Benny stared at the path. It went straight into the darkest part of the forest. He had never been that way before, not even on a bright and sunny day. Could he really do it now, in the rain and mud and thunder?

BOOM.

Thump-thump-thump.

Flip-flop.

Benny almost turned around and ran home, but that wouldn't fix anything. He had to find the magic wishing tree and make everything go back to normal.

With his mind made up, Benny hurried down the dark path, deep into the forest.

The trees that lined the path were tall, and they leaned toward each other so that their leafy branches blocked most of the rain. But the path was still muddy, and Benny had to climb over rocks and fallen branches and wade through puddles, which were so deep they were almost ponds.

BOOM.

Thump-thump-thump! Flip-flop!

'Are you okay?' said someone.

Benny's heart was racing. First, he thought he'd imagined the voice. Then he looked up and saw a robin perched on a branch.

'I'm fine,' Benny said, even though his heart was still thump-thumping, and his stomach was still flip-flopping. 'My name is Benny. What's yours?'

'I'm Ruby,' said the robin. 'Are you sure you're okay? You look really scared!'

Embarrassed, Benny started to shake his head. Then he realised Ruby wasn't laughing at him.

'Well, thunder kind of scares me,' he admitted. 'Every time it goes BOOM, my heart beats too fast and my stomach flips over!'

Ruby nodded. 'I know just what you mean. Every time the wind howls through the trees, all my feathers stand straight up. It looks so silly!'

'Why does the wind scare you?' Benny asked.

'The howl sounds like a monster,' Ruby replied. 'I know it's not really a monster. But it still scares me anyway! I do wish this storm

would end soon.'

'Me too!' Benny said excitedly. 'There's a magic wishing tree down this path. I'm going to find it and make a wish that the storm had never happened!'

'Wow!' Ruby exclaimed. 'Can I come along?'

'Yes!'

They set off down the path together. Ruby flew alongside Benny. Suddenly, a gust of wind blew through the trees.

OoooOOOOOOOOOOooooooooh!

Poof!

All of Ruby's feathers stood on end. She looked like a fluffy ball instead of a robin. But Benny didn't laugh at her.

'Are you okay?' he asked.

Ruby closed her eyes and began talking out loud to herself. 'Everyone gets scared. Fear is just a feeling. It's okay to feel fear sometimes.'

Benny watched her curiously. 'What are you doing?'

'That's what I do when I get scared or worried,' she told him. 'I just say things to myself to help me feel better.'

Benny thought about how Ruby's kind words helped her with her fear. It was quite different from the thoughts Benny usually had when he was scared. He thought: this is so

BOOM.

Again, Benny leapt up high in the air.

Thump-thump-thump!
Flip-flop!

He landed in the mud and
crouched there, trembling.

But Ruby wasn't laughing at him.

'Fear is just a feeling,' she said again. 'Now you try!'

Benny decided to try. He said to himself, 'Fear is just a feeling. It's okay to be scared sometimes.'

To his surprise, he stopped trembling. He did feel a little better!

'Thanks, Ruby,' he said with a smile.

Eventually, the path led them past a pond overflowing with rainwater. A bright green frog drifted towards them on a lily pad.

'Hello, there!' the frog called out. 'My name's Freddie.'

'Hi, Freddie,' 'I'm Benny, and this is my friend Ruby.'

'Nice to meet you,' Freddie said. 'But why are you two out in this storm?'

But before Benny or Ruby could respond, lightning flashed across the sky. And then...

BOOM.

OoooOOOOOOOOOooooooooh!

Thump-thump-thump! Flip-flop!

Poof!

Benny closed his eyes. 'Fear is just a feeling,' he said to himself. Next to him, he could hear Ruby whispering the very same thing.

When he opened his eyes, he was surprised to see Freddie's belly was suddenly like a big, round bubble. Benny and Ruby watched as Freddie breathed out, and his belly shrank back to normal. He breathed in again, and his belly grew and grew...then whoosh! He let out his breath and his belly shrank.

Freddie opened his eyes and smiled when he saw them staring. 'Lightning frightens me sometimes, so I belly breathe.'

'What's belly breathing?' Ruby asked.

'I take a big, deep breath in and count to three in my head,' Freddie explained. 'The breath goes all the way down to my belly. Then I hold it there and count to three before letting it out again. I do it as many times as I need to until I start to feel calmer. Want to try it?'

'Yes!' Benny said eagerly. His heart was still racing from the thunder.

Together, the three of them breathed in for three counts. Benny felt his own belly bulging, just like Freddie's. Then they held it for three counts before breathing out.

Ruby smiled. 'I feel a lot better!'

'Me too!' Benny said. 'Freddie, we're on our way to the magic wishing tree. I'm going to make a wish that this storm never happened. Want to come along?'

'I'd love to!' Freddie said.

They headed down the path. Ruby flew alongside Benny, while Freddie hopped on his other side. Eventually, they came to a little clearing. It reminded Benny of his glade, only this one wasn't flooded, but it was filled with piles of sopping wet leaves.

'Wheeeeee!'

'This is so much fun!'

'Watch how high I can hop!'

Benny, Ruby and Freddie stopped and stared. A family of bunnies was frolicking in the leaves!

'Hi there!' A bunny hopped over and smiled at them. 'I'm Bella.'

'Hi, Bella,' said Benny. 'I'm Benny, and these are my friends Ruby and Freddie.'

'Nice to meet you!' Bella said. 'Would you like to come and play with us?'

Suddenly, lightning flashed
Across the sky.
And then:

BOOM.

OoooOOOOOOOOOOooooooooh!

Thump-thump-thump! Flip-flop!

Poof!

Benny closed his eyes. 'Fear is just a feeling,' he whispered. Then he belly breathed. He could hear Ruby and Freddie doing the same thing.

'Thanks,' he said finally, looking at Bella. 'I would love to play, but I can't have fun while this storm is going on! It has ruined everything.

Bella's ears twitched. "That's a shame, the storm ruined our play place too, but then we found this one. So long as we're together, we can have fun anywhere!"

Benny smiled at her. But deep down, he just wanted everything to go back to the way it was before the storm. "We're going to find the magic wishing tree," he told Bella. "Want to come?"

"That sounds like fun!" Bella said. The four friends set off down the path together. Through the mud and over slippery logs and big rocks, they chatted about the forest and the storm and their fears. Benny was so distracted, he actually forgot to feel afraid.

"Look!" Ruby cried suddenly.

"The magic wishing tree!"

'Wow.' Benny stopped and stared at the tree in amazement. It was magnificent, with a strong, thick trunk and green leaves that

'We found it!' Bella cheered.

'Go on, Benny!' Freddie said. 'Make your wish.'

Benny stepped forward and took a deep breath.

'I wish that this terrible storm had never happened!'

Silence fell. He waited for the rain to stop and the sun to come out, and all the fallen trees to stand up and plant their roots back in the ground.

But nothing happened.

'Why isn't it working?' Bella wondered aloud.

'Make the wish again, Benny!' Ruby suggested.

Then another voice spoke up.

'It doesn't work like that.'

Benny and his friends looked up. Ollie the owl had appeared on one of the branches of the magic wishing tree!

'What do you mean, Ollie?' Benny asked.

'As I said before, this tree will grant you what you need,' Ollie explained, 'not necessarily what you want. What you want is for this storm to never have happened…but wishes can only go forward, not backward. You needed to find out this truth for yourself!'

BOOM.

Thump-thump-thump! Flip-flop!

Benny took a deep breath into his belly, then breathed out. 'Fear is just a feeling,' he murmured to himself.

Ollie was smiling at him. 'I know you want this storm to end, Benny,' he said softly. 'We all do. And we might not know when that will happen, but all storms do end eventually.'

'If you knew all of that already, why did you send me on this quest?' Benny asked. 'I'm so scared of thunder!'

'You are?' Bella asked. 'And you went out in the storm anyway? Wow, Benny, you're really brave!'

Benny was surprised. 'I am? Being scared of thunder always made me feel worried!'

'We all feel scared sometimes,' Bella said. 'But you were also brave enough to do something about it, and help yourself by going out to find the magic wishing tree! And to be honest, I'm glad your wish didn't come true.'

'You are?' Benny blinked. 'But why?'

Bella grinned. 'Because storms do happen, and if this one had never happened, none of us would have met!'

'She's right!' Ruby exclaimed.

'I didn't even think of that!' Freddie agreed.

'See, Benny?' Ollie said. 'This quest was worth it after all!'

'You're right,' Benny admitted, a smile spreading on his face. 'Besides, thanks to Ruby, now I know how to say kind things to help make myself feel better. And I learned how to belly breathe, thanks to Freddie. And Bella showed me that even if my favourite place to play is gone, I can still have fun!'

'That's right!' Ollie looked pleased. 'Of course, you still have a wish to make, if you want to.'

Benny gazed at the shimmering leaves on the magic wishing tree. He closed his eyes and made his wish.

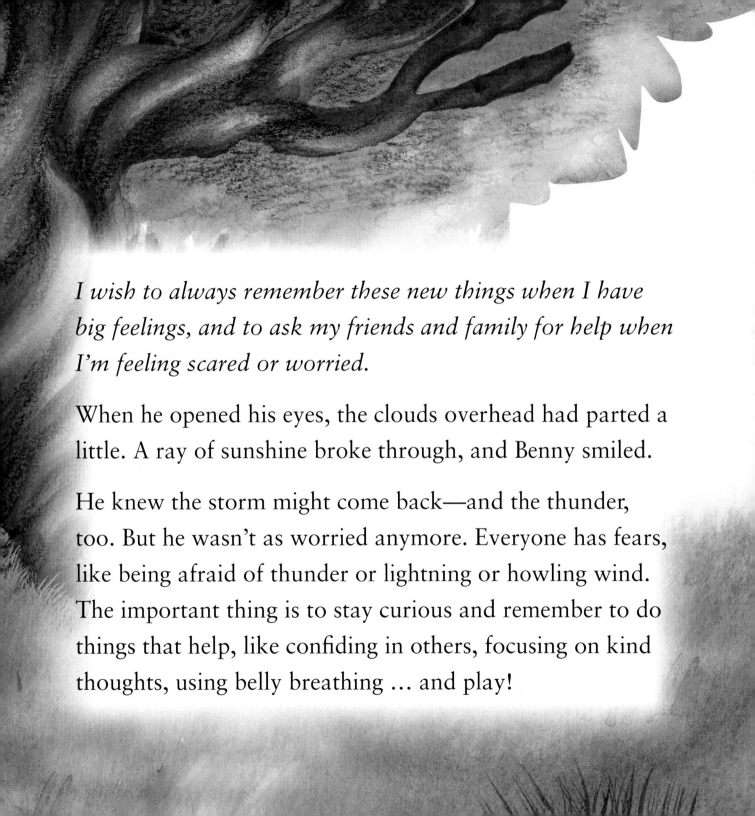

I wish to always remember these new things when I have big feelings, and to ask my friends and family for help when I'm feeling scared or worried.

When he opened his eyes, the clouds overhead had parted a little. A ray of sunshine broke through, and Benny smiled.

He knew the storm might come back—and the thunder, too. But he wasn't as worried anymore. Everyone has fears, like being afraid of thunder or lightning or howling wind. The important thing is to stay curious and remember to do things that help, like confiding in others, focusing on kind thoughts, using belly breathing … and play!

'I have to go.' Benny said, turning to head down the path.

'You're leaving!' Ruby exclaimed.

'Why?' Freddie asked.

'Come and play with us!' Bella added.

Benny turned and smiled at his new friends.

'I will. But first I want to find Sammy and my parents and bring them here. This is the perfect new play place!'

His friends cheered, and Benny waved as he set off for home. He couldn't wait to tell his family all about his adventure.

Dear Reader

I hope you enjoyed reading about Benny's adventure!
I am a child & adult psychotherapist who specialises in creative techniques.
This book was written to help children express and process big feelings
through the story of Benny, as he navigates change, loss and anxiety.

Please visit my website www.drvharris.com for a link to downloadable
activities, that can further help your child explore and gain confidence
with their feelings and emotions.

I'd love to hear from you and would really appreciate it if you could leave a review on
Amazon. Your views are important. It will help me to develop new books for children,
and assist in making Benny's story reach those who need it most!

Much love,

Dr. Victoria Harris